# CALLING IT A DAY

## A SECURITY DIRECTORATE SHORT STORY

### ALEXANDRIA BLAELOCK

# Also by Alexandria Blaelock

SHORT STORY COLLECTIONS
The Histories of Hayward Hall
Lovelorn, Lovestruck and Love at First Sight
Common or Garden Variety Heroes
Case Files of the Wilkinson Detective Agency
Unavoidable Fates
Christmas Travesties
Five Faces of Felicia Clarke
Little Place Called Home

FICTION
That Love Nonsense
Taipan vs Brown
The Ghost and Ms Cox
Friends Like That

MS BLAELOCK'S BOOKS
Stress Free Dinner Parties
Signature Wardrobe Planning
Holistic Personal Finance
Minimally Viable Housekeeping
Planning a Life Worth Living

A SELECTION OF AVAILABLE SHORT STORIES
Alma's Grace
Fate in Your Hands
Lady of the Looking Glass
Morning Star, Evening Star, Superstar
Secret Singer
Shining Star
Ship in a Bottle
Simone Says Hands in the Air
The Day the Schedule Broke

# CALLING IT A DAY

## A SECURITY DIRECTORATE SHORT STORY

ALEXANDRIA BLAELOCK

BlueMere Books
MELBOURNE, AUSTRALIA

For permission requests, please contact
enquiries@bluemerebooks.com.

Ordering Information:
Discounts are available on quantity purchases. For details, contact orders@bluemerebooks.com.

Calling it a Day/Alexandria Blaelock
paperback ISBN: 978-1-922744-84-5
digital ISBN: 978-1-922744-85-2

Book Layout © BookDesignTemplates.com
Cover Art © khius/Depositphotos

BlueMere Books
www.bluemerebooks.com

# CALLING IT A DAY

The phone box was red.

She wanted to call it pillar box red, but did not know where the words came from. Or what they meant - what was a pillar box?

The box had a domed top with four walls made of small glass panes. Six tall, three wide, set into wood beading, all painted red, and joined at the corners with lines of vertically striped moulding.

Like a stick of rock candy, though she did not know what those words meant or where they came from either.

The box didn't have a phone inside it, but above the door was a sign that said telephone, surmounted by a moulded crown.

She had an urge to curl her blue gloved fingers under the elegant domed handle and pull the door open.

The box made her feel light and bouncy.

As if there should be laughing.

And skipping.

And the taste of sweetness in her mouth.

Her hair in bouncy puppy dog tails hanging over her ears.

The feeling was as unusual as it was unexpected and set her nerves on fire.

She didn't know where it came from, or why it was so different from the darkness she usually felt.

It was disturbing.

And uncomfortable.

It made her regulation chignon feel too tight, and the weight of her uniform cap too heavy.

Captain Maeryn Prothero turned her back on the perplexing box and looked out over the junk yard her unit was currently searching.

That was more like it. The cold application of logic to the problem at hand, and fortunately, her career had progressed far enough that it was no longer her hands combing the site for evidence.

Her job was to direct the search, analyse the results, and arrest the guilty.

She shoved her hands in the pockets of her navy-blue greatcoat so she wasn't tempted to mess with her hair, annoyed she felt the need.

Both to mess her hair *and* to restrain herself.

A Eugenics Programme success, she'd passed the Genomics Bureau post-natal testing, survived the State Academy of Cultural Regulation with a useful genetic "superpower" and graduated from the University of Civilisation with an advantageous qualification.

All so long ago, she barely remembered it.

It was a very long time since she'd taken her first posting at the Bureau of Internal Investigations, yet here she was, losing her cool like a newbie to an inanimate object.

In a swirl of greatcoat tails, she stalked a few paces away so the box couldn't see her, and instantly felt better.

She barked a few orders at the goons and felt better still.

That was more like her, not to mention she had a hard-arse reputation to maintain.

Actually, being a hard-arse was her "superpower," a genetic gift courtesy of the Security Directorate Eugenics Program.

Always assuming you thought extreme impassivity was a gift, but it made her good at hunting out and executing traitors.

A gift that almost, but not quite, made up for her unusually angular, darkly hirsute ugliness. Not to mention the ridiculously witchy wart on her nose she hadn't got around to removing yet.

She'd never failed to solve a case, and she'd never failed a mission.

Incredibly, she found her thoughts returning to the box.

Was it possible someone had the kind of "superpower" that might allow them to add something to an inanimate object to repel the curious? Would it work on the marginally gifted and normals as well?

Should someone actually have such a power, to use it without the proper authorisation was treasonous.

She'd have it sent back to the lab and get it checked out.

A small, delicate woman approached and waited for acknowledgement.

"Simms," Prothero nodded.

"Ma'am," she saluted, and Prothero sketched a reply.

"We've searched the offices and car yard, and nothing so far."

Prothero grunted. Simms' shoulders started turning away, but immediately swivelled back when her boss cleared her throat.

"There's something bothering me about the phone box," she said, pointing a thumb over her shoulder, "have it sent back to the lab with whatever else you find."

"Yes Ma'am."

"I'll head back now. Let me know when you get in."

"Ma'am."

Prothero turned and walked away, back to the car, catching her driver by surprise. She didn't bother reprimanding him, just climbed in, leaving him scrambling to catch up.

«« • »»

The wait for information about the phone box was tedious.

She immersed herself in reviewing the progress of ongoing investigations.

She visited the warehouses to inspect the relevant evidences, but they were an excuse to visit the box. To prowl around it, hands clasped behind her back, fascinated yet repelled by it.

Technicians had analysed the manufacturing materials.

Sensitives had examined it for evidence of superpower application.

There was absolutely nothing to suggest there was anything out of the ordinary about it.

It was exactly what it appeared to be.

And yet she couldn't let it go.

«« • »»

When the psych evaluation reminder popped up on her screen, she was ludicrously relieved and immediately left her desk.

In general, she believed the mandatory quarterly evaluations were critical for the ongoing efficiency of everyone at a lower rank than captain.

In her line of work, investigators were regularly exposed to the worst of the worst, and it was essential to ensure none of her operatives were suborned in any way.

But at her level, with her security clearance, they were a waste of time.

Normally she'd reschedule them until they threatened her with disciplinary action before attending.

But this time, the idea of hoops to jump through was a welcome distraction.

In the blindingly white clinical rooms, Dr Kov's receptionist was so surprised to see her she couldn't string together a coherent sentence.

Prothero ignored her, ignoring the white plastic chairs and cheery motivational posters, pacing up and down the waiting area until she was called into his retro wood panelled rooms.

Still restless, she shoved her hands into her pockets and threw herself onto the patient couch. A surprisingly comfortable kind of scuffed tan leather sling supported by a curved chrome cradle resting on a blackened metal stand.

"So Prothero," he said, swivelling his chair away from his no nonsense wooden desk to look at her, "what's on your mind?"

"What makes you think there's something on my mind?"

"You're here aren't you? You haven't tried to reschedule even once."

She slumped lower into the couch, "ah."

"Shall we do the usual dance Captain, or seeing as you're here more or less willingly, shall we get straight to the nub of the matter?"

Prothero closed her eyes and screwed her face up, like a child forced to eat green vegetables.

"Yes, I can suspend you, but my job is to take care of you, so you can take care of the Directorate. Rest assured, I won't be doing that unless I think you're a danger to yourself and others."

"Fine." She sighed, "we were searching a junk yard for evidence, and we found a phone box. And the idea of it makes me uncomfortable."

"I see, and why do you think that is."

"I don't know. There's nothing to suggest it is in any way unusual, but I can't stop thinking about it."

"How mysterious. Do you have a theory?"

"I'm not sure. I wondered if it was significant in some way, but I don't recall seeing anything like it before."

"The Directorate is experimenting with a hypnosis treatment modality. Would you like me to seek authorisation to add you to the program?"

"Hypnosis? What does that involve?"

"Well, used as a treatment for trauma, it helps to dissociate the trauma and remodel the experiences more positively."

"And what makes you think it might help me and the phone box?"

"It might be possible to recover experiences you've forgotten or blocked out, and reintegrate them into your psyche."

"Reintegrate what now?"

"Just think of it as resolving your issues."

"Okay. But will it work?"

"There's a good chance it will make things better, but there's a slight chance it'll make your situation worse."

"Aahhh. Okay.

"Let's do it then."

Kov cleared his throat, "right. Well. Given the secure nature of the work you undertake, I need to get permission to try it on you. You may get permission to receive the treatment, but I may be required to pass you onto a different therapist."

"I'm not sure I'm comfortable with that."

"Well, let's seek permission and see what comes back."

Prothero growled.

"How long will that take?"

"Shouldn't be more than a day or two, I wouldn't think."

"Fine fine fine. Let's do that."

"I'll call you when I know more."

«« • »»

In fact, it was almost a week before Prothero heard anything further.

The week included a series of gruelling court-martial testimonies, followed by a death sentence, and performing the resulting execution.

So when the notice of the appointment with Kov came, she was pleased to see it.

Without question, she took the offered sedative and made herself comfortable on the sling couch.

She followed Kov's prompts, and before long found herself in a different universe.

Running along a beach.

The sun was setting on her left in a blaze of orange and purple; the vibrancy of the sky was turning the clear blue water into shades of grey, and the yellow sand a darker grey.

To her right, grasses grew in clumps, but she was trying not to look because someone was chasing her.

Her head was down as she pumped her tiny arms and legs.

They were on fire with pain, and she wasn't sure how much longer she could keep running.

Her breath was getting stuck in her lungs as she tried to gasp it out and breathe in fresh.

It didn't matter.

She had to keep running because if she stopped, something bad would happen.

Someone grabbed her shoulder, and she screamed, high and sharp and shrill.

Dr Kov said something, and her mind went blank.

He said something else, and she saw a red phone box.

It was very tall, or perhaps she was very small.

The sun was high in the sky, and she was sitting on a bench on the other side of the road, swinging her legs backwards and forwards as she watched the people walk by.

Her father nudged her with his elbow, and she giggled and tossed her head, making the twin hair tails hanging over her ears swing in the light breeze from the ocean.

She licked chocolate ice cream from the top of her cone, then licked the melting ice cream from her hand and the bottom of the cone, racing to eat it all before the cone dissolved.

He nudged her again, and she jumped off the bench, taking his hand as they walked across the road, onto the pier.

He played some kind of shooting game, and she cheered and clapped and dropped her ice cream and started crying.

He won her a small white teddy bear, then bought her a stick of hard peppermint flavoured rock. Red on the outside, and white on the inside, with some words she couldn't read on the inside. He unwrapped one end for her and stole a lick or two for quality control before he gave it to her to try.

It was so sweet it made her tongue curl.

She loved it.

Joy flooded her tiny body as thoroughly as the sugar from the rock.

They followed the sound of tinny music to a carousel at the end of the pier. He put her on a snow-white horse with a gold mane and turquoise livery and waved at her as she passed him.

She laughed and waved back and swore to herself she would remember this day forever.

And then she came around again, and Daddy was nowhere to be seen.

"Daddy?" she called, but there was no answer.

She stood as high as the stirrups would allow, scanning the crowd as the carousel made another circuit before slowing and stopping.

"Daddy?" she cried a little louder, running for the exit, turning around and around looking for him.

And then she saw him, dragged away by big men wearing black.

So she ran down the pier as fast as her legs could carry her, screaming "Daddy" as she chased them off the end and along the street.

Still running, still screaming, as she watched the men bundle him into a black van.

Still screaming as one of them turned and started running towards her.

She closed her mouth, wheeled silently and ran away, across the road, and down along the sand.

Kov said something, and her mind went blank.

He said some other things, and her breathing and heart rate slowed.

He said some more, and she drifted into a gentle sleep.

«« • »»

When she woke, she was back in her tiny one-room flat. The one allocated for her first posting and she'd never got round to applying for something else.

With just enough room for a bed and a chair. On one wall, next to a glass doored Juliet balcony overlooking the seafront, a cupboard housing a sink and a one burner electric stove. And on the other, next to the blue entry door, one shelf with a hanging rack.

A little disoriented, not knowing how she got there.

But calm.

She remembered seeing Dr Kov, taking a pill, and going to sleep.

Then nothing.

She assumed she'd passed her psych evaluation and was grateful to have got out of that bureaucratic nightmare unscathed.

She poured herself a glass of wine, opened the door, and leaned on the Juliet balcony railing as she looked down and out, over the sparkling water, taking deep breaths of the fresh sea air.

After a moment, she realised she was hungry, but chose to lean her elbows on the balcony and enjoy the view a little longer.

It had been a long week.

There was plenty of time for a stroll along the seafront, and for sharing some fish and chips with the seagulls.

As she turned back to the room, a grey, threadbare stuffed toy caught her eye. She frowned at it, trying to remember where it came from, or why she had it.

She shook her head as she picked it up and dropped it in the bin on her way out the door.

Life was hard enough without filling her house up with old rubbish.

**THE END**

# ABOUT THE AUTHOR

Alexandria Blaelock writes stories, some of them for *Ellery Queen's Mystery Magazine* and *Pulphouse Fiction Magazine*.

She's also written five selfhelp books applying business techniques to personal matters like getting dressed, cleaning house, and feeding your friends.

She lives in a forest because she enjoys birdsong, and the smell of gum leaves. When not telecommuting to parallel universes from her Melbourne based imagination, she watches K-dramas, talks to animals, and drinks Campari. At the same time.
Discover more at www.alexandriablaelock.com.

# IF YOU ENJOYED THIS STORY...

try the other Security Directorate stories

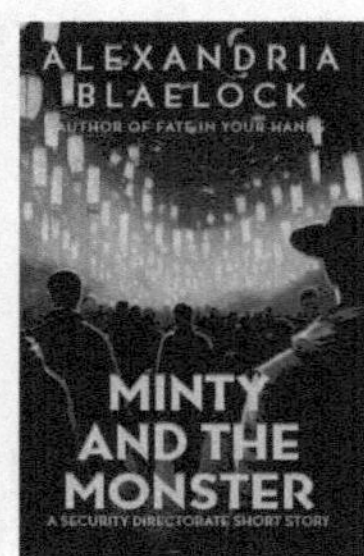

... or the collections

Why not try The Ghost and Ms Cox

**Life interrupted**

To say the letter was a surprise was an understatement. It arrived addressed to Miss Finlay Cox, which made the contents even more extraordinary.

Orphan Finn Cox inherits a cottage. Thinks it holds the key to her origins. Of course she takes a look. Who wouldn't?

But when she gets there, she gets more than she bargained for.

Is it friend, family or foe?